Bark, Spike, Bark!

SIMON SPOTLIGHT
An imprint of Simon & Schuster Children's Publishing Division
1230 Avenue of the Americas
New York, New York 10020

Based on the TV series *Rugrats*® created by Klasky/Csupo Inc. and
Paul Germain as seen on Nickelodeon®

First Simon Spotlight Edition, 1998

Manufactured in the United States of America
10 9 8 7 6 5 4 3 2 1

Library of Congress Cataloging-in-Publication Data
David, Luke.
Bark, Spike, bark! / by Luke David ; illustrated by George Ulrich. — 1st ed.
p.   cm. — (Ready-to-read)
Summary: Chuckie and Tommy misconstrue Stu's efforts at car repair with
"bark plugs" as an attempt to silence the family dog.
"Based on the TV series Rugrats created by Klasky/Csupo Inc. and Paul
Germain as seen on Nickelodeon"—p. [4] of cover.
ISBN 0-689-82129-8 (pb)
[1. Babies—Fiction. 2. Dogs—Fiction. 3. Automobiles—Maintenance and
repair—Fiction.] I. Ulrich, George, ill. II. Title. III. Series.
PZ7.A37735Bar   1998
97-44204
[Fic]—dc21
CIP   AC

By Luke David
Illustrated by George Ulrich

Ready-to-Read

Simon Spotlight/Nickelodeon

One morning, Tommy's dad Stu was fixing his car. Tommy and Chuckie played with the tools in the toolbox.

A chipmunk dashed across the lawn. Spike spotted it.

"*Woof-woof*," barked Spike. "*Woof-woof-woof-woof-WOOF-WOOF!*"

He chased the chipmunk around and around a tree.

"Put a plug in it, Spike!" yelled Stu. "You're hurting my ears. Your bark is loud! TOO loud!"

But Spike just kept barking.

Stu sighed. He went back to fixing the car. Suddenly, he slammed down the hood.

"C'mon, kids," he said. "We have to get some spark plugs!"

"Bark plugs!" said Tommy in the car. "Dad wants to stop Spike from barking. That's not fair! Chuckie, we have to do something!"

"I don't know, Tommy," said Chuckie.

Stu parked the car.

"But Spike loves to bark," continued Tommy, "just like we love to laugh and cry and stomp our feet and bang our toy hammers against the TV! When Spike barks, it's because he has something to say!"

Stu carried the boys into the store.

"And besides," said Tommy, "you wouldn't like it very much if someone put a plug in your mouth!"

"Well, okay, Tommy," Chuckie said. "I guess I'll help you. But I don't want any trouble."

13

"Don't worry," answered Tommy. He looked around the store. "It'll be easy. We just have to find all the bark plugs and hide them! Then Dad won't be able to buy any."

Stu put the boys down. "Wow, look at those shocks and struts," he said. "They're computerized!"

With his dad's back turned, Tommy
took off down the aisle. "C'mon, Chuckie,"
he said. "We've got some bark plugs
to find!"

"Aaaargh!" said Chuckie. "Maybe these are the bark plugs! Maybe your Dad will wrap that cord around Spike's snout and snap those clips on his ears!"

"Nah," said Tommy. "Those are rooster cables for the car. Dad uses them when the car is sleeping. The cables make the rooster inside the hood crow, so the car wakes up and goes again."

"What about these jugs, Tommy?" asked Chuckie. "Maybe they're full of medicine, and your Dad will give some to Spike to make him stop barking!"

"Nuh-hunh," said Tommy. "That stuff is also for the car. It's anti-sneeze. Dad pours it in the engine when it has a cold so the car stops sneezing."

Just then, the babies heard a lady
yell "Bingo!"

"Here are the spark plugs!" she said.

They followed the lady's voice. "C'mon,
Chuckie," said Tommy, "we've got some
hiding to do!"

The babies climbed up on the shelf and pushed all the spark plugs deep into the bottom of a bin.

Tommy saw his dad talking to the man at the counter. "Okay, I'll take your word for it," said Stu, "no need for new spark plugs."

Tommy gave Chuckie a high-five. "Yaaaaay! We did it. Spike will bark again!"

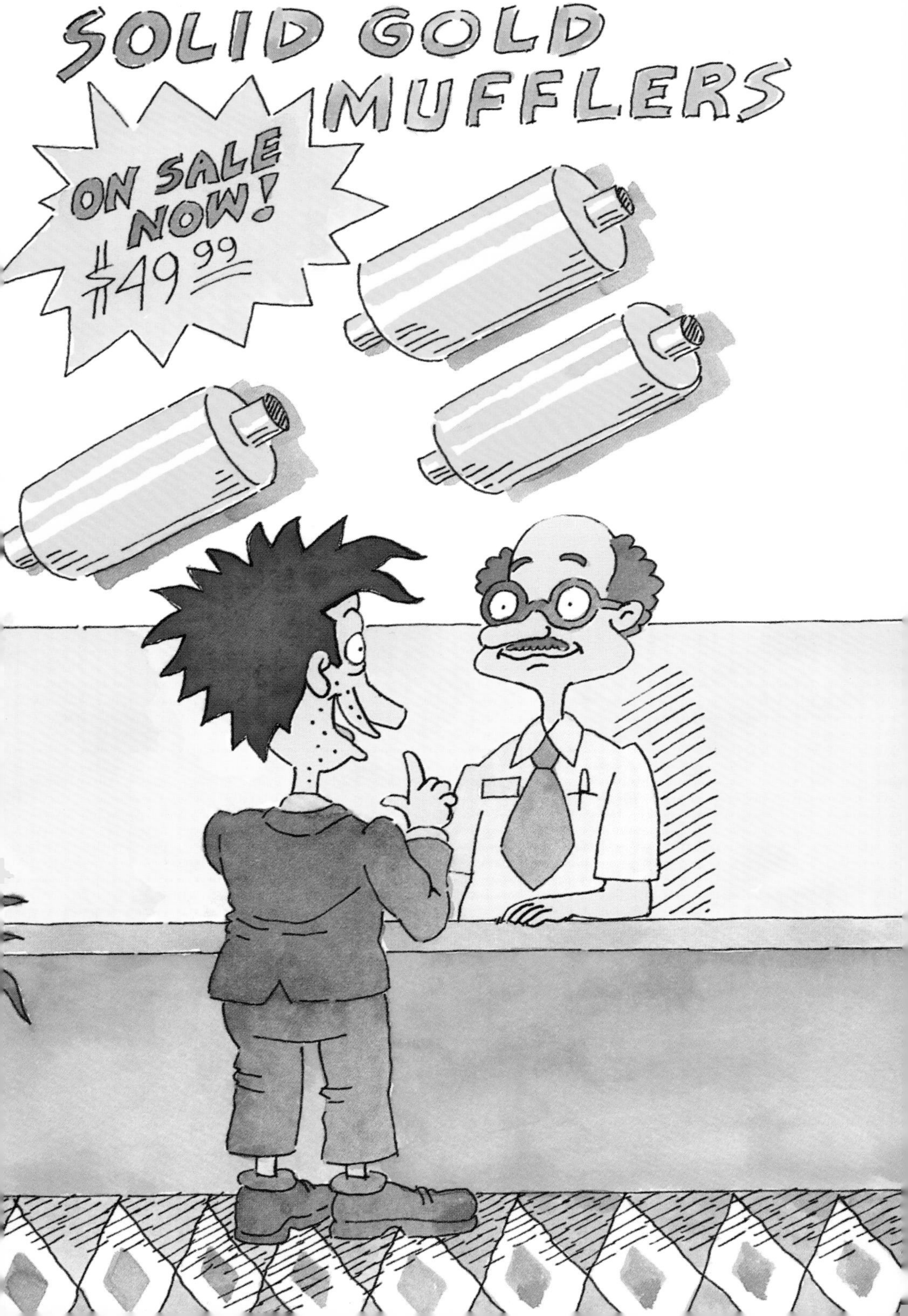
SOLID GOLD MUFFLERS
ON SALE NOW!
$49.99

Stu said, "So there's a sale on the solid gold mufflers? All right, twist my arm. I'll take one. What a beauty!"

Spike was happy to see them when they got back in the car. He barked. Stu drove them home.

"Spike is doomed, doomed, doomed!" said Chuckie. "Your dad is going to muffler him. And he'll never bark again!"

"Don't worry. We'll think of something," said Tommy. "We saved him from the bark plugs, didn't we?"

At home, Stu took the boys out of
the car. He let out Spike. Then Stu took out
the muffler. He started walking toward Spike.

"NOOOOO!" screamed Chuckie.

"CHARGE!" yelled Tommy. He and
Chuckie raced toward Stu.

But Stu walked past Spike.

"Look, Chuckie," said Tommy. "Dad's going to muffler the car instead of Spike! Now Spike can still bark. Yaaaaaaay!"

Stu took the old muffler off the car and put on the new one.

Then Stu looked at Tommy and Chuckie. "Aw, shucks, boys," he said. "I haven't paid enough attention to you two today. I bet car repair isn't exactly your idea of fun! So let's have some! Fun, I mean."

Stu took the boys to the backyard.

Stu put Tommy and Chuckie in the swings. He pushed them back and forth.

Spike chased another chipmunk up a tree. "*Woof-woof-woof-WOOF-WOOF!*"

But Tommy and Chuckie were fast asleep. Not even Spike's bark could wake them!